ISBN 0-86163-499-3

Copyright © 1991 Award Publications Limited

First published 1991 by Award Publications Limited,
Spring House, Spring Place,
Kentish Town, London NW5 3BH

Printed in Germany

Henry's Wagon

by

Peg Dikeman

AWARD PUBLICATIONS

HENRY'S WAGON

Sometimes Henry would put on his Indian suit and his hat with the tall red feathers. Then he would play that his wagon was a canoe and he'd paddle away looking for a fish to cook in his wigwam.

Whenever his mother said he could, Henry would put the garden hose in his wagon and race down the walk as fast as he could yelling, "Dang! Dang! Make way for this big fire chief."

Yes, wagons certainly were lots of fun.

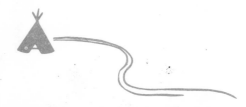

Henry had a beautiful red wagon which he loved better than any other toy in the whole wide world

BECAUSE—

he could play train with his wagon. He'd put his Panda, his real live dog, Skippie, and his nice stuffed giraffe in the wagon—

and then—

Henry would be the conductor. After he'd given his passengers their tickets, he'd run down the sidewalk yelling, "All Aboard! Choo! Choo! Choo!"

One day while Henry was out playing with his wagon, he got so hungry that he ran into the house to get a glass of milk and a ginger-snap

AND

he left his nice red wagon in the yard. Usually he was very careful to put it in the garage, but this time he forgot, which was unfortunate

BECAUSE

Pretty soon nice smiling Mr. Sun went sailing away behind a cloud to take a nap.

And in a few minutes,
PITTER PATTER, the big rain—
drops began to splash
all over HENRY'S
PRETTY RED WAGON

Now, RAIN, as everyone knows

        is good for the GRASS

           and the FLOWERS

            and the TREES

and DUCKS and TURTLES and sometimes even RABBITS like rain too!

            BUT

Rain is NOT very good for wagons.

    In a very few days, the pretty red paint
began to crack and peel off Henry's wagon.

Henry was very unhappy when he saw his nice red wagon with the paint all gone, because it wasn't pretty any more. He ran to find his mother.

"Mother," said Henry, "will you paint my wagon for me, please?"

His mother said she would, but she was feeding the kittens, and she forgot all about it.

Henry was disappointed because his mother forgot to paint his wagon so he went to the kitchen to see Bessie, the nice smiling cook.

"Bessie," he said, "will you please paint my wagon for me?"

But Bessie was busy making cookies, and told him to run along and play.

Just then Dick and Sue, who lived next door, came skating down the walk.

"Hi there!" called Henry. "Could you paint my wagon for me?"

But Dick and Sue said they had to go to school.

Feeling very sad indeed, Henry wandered over to watch the man who was working in the yard.

He thought perhaps *he* would paint his wagon, but the gardener was too busy cutting grass.

Henry was so unhappy that he sat down on the steps in front of his house and told Skippie all about it. He tried very hard not to cry because BIG boys don't cry—very often.

Just then Henry saw a painter down the street painting a garage. As fast as his legs could carry him, he ran down there to watch.

The painter would dip his big brush into the bucket and, SLAP, SLAP, back and forth, on would go the green paint.

It looked as if it would be fun, thought Henry—and easy, too.

When the painter was through, he came down the ladder and Henry asked him if he could have the rest of the paint for his wagon.

The painter gave it to him, and Henry was very happy again.

He sat down on the ground and dipped his finger in the paint. It came out green and when he rubbed it on the wagon it made a pretty green stripe.

"This is fun," said Henry.

Then Henry dipped his whole hand into the bucket of green paint and rubbed it back and forth along the wagon. That was fun too, but still pretty slow.

"Guess I'll use both hands," said Henry.

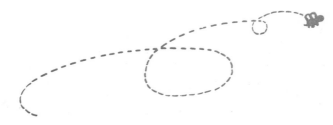

That was fine and much faster.
He painted the SIDES
  and the WHEELS
   and the SEAT
    and the HANDLE
Just as he finished, a big fly came buzz-buZZ-BUZZING around his head. Henry brushed him off with his green hands and his hair felt wet and sticky.

But he didn't care because his wagon was GREEN ALL OVER.

Calling, "Here, Skippie! Here Skippie!" he proudly grabbed his wagon and said, "Let's go home and show our wagon to Bessie."

When he got to the kitchen window he said "Hi, Bessie! Please come outdoors right now and see my wagon. I painted it all by MYSELF—AND—

—Bessie,
I'm a LITTLE
MESSY."